Oswald
and
Friends
in the Forest of
Hidden Secrets

A Surprise Visit!

JULIE SPIBY

AuthorHouse™ UK
1663 Liberty Drive
Bloomington, IN 47403 USA
www.authorhouse.co.uk
UK TFN: 0800 0148641 (Toll Free inside the UK)
UK Local: 02036 956322 (+44 20 3695 6322 from outside the UK)

This book is printed on acid-free paper.

ISBN: 978-1-7283-7511-3 (sc)
ISBN: 978-1-7283-7512-0 (e)

Print information available on the last page.

Published by AuthorHouse 09/28/2022

authorHOUSE®

Oswald
and
Friends
in the Forest of
Hidden Secrets

A Surprise Visit!

It was a cold, bright and sunny morning. Oswald the mighty oak tree was looking over the forest of hidden secrets. He felt happy as he watched the other trees, animals, insects and plants all enjoying the lovely Autumn sunshine. Oswald loved the Autumn. He was always amazed how the trees' leaves changed their colours so beautifully and how different his forest looked when the seasons changed each year.

Suddenly, Oswald felt a tingling sensation. His leaves began to quiver on his branches. "Oh!" thought Oswald, "I have a message". The message was coming from the trees on the outer rim of the forest, through their leaves, in their secret tree language. Oswald concentrated very hard so he could understand what the trees were trying to tell him.

"People" he said to himself, "We haven't seen any people for ages, I wonder why they are visiting our forest?"

Now, Oswald was not just an ordinary tree, he was King of the forest, a wise old tree, and he had been alive for hundreds of years. He knew that the forest was meant to be shared. Using the same secret tree language, he sent a message back through his leaves to the other trees' leaves, explaining that they should wait and see what happens next.

Soon, the visitors' voices could be heard as they walked towards the middle of the forest. They were talking about ideas for playing and learning in the forest. After quite a long time, the visitors left the forest.

Oswald knew that all the trees, animals and insects in the forest would be very curious about their visitors. He decided to call a meeting. Oswald took a deep breath and blew into one of his branches. The branch quivered slightly, then ever so slowly turned into a musical instrument. It made the most beautiful noise. It sounded like a choir of fairies singing as it floated out over the forest of hidden secrets. All the animals and insects stopped what they were doing instantly. They all knew that the beautiful sound meant Oswald wanted everybody in the forest to come to the log circle in the centre of the forest. They all rushed as quickly as they could.

When everyone had assembled Oswald told them that he knew all about the visitors and that he had heard them talking about how children could play and learn in the forest.

"But what will they learn by playing in our forest?" asked Reya Rabbit.

"Well" said Oswald, "we know the forest is a magical place and maybe our forest is something that might help children play and learn all sorts of new things and have lots of fun outside".

"Don't humans live outside?" asked Melissa mouse.

"No", said Oswald, "they live in houses".

"What are houses?" asked Sammy squirrel.

"Houses are where humans live together, they eat and sleep in houses which protects them from heat, cold and bad weather." replied Oswald.

"So, they are different to us" said Squirrel.

"Every living creature is different. Humans don't build a drey in a tree like you do squirrel, or a burrow underground like you do rabbit. They build houses out of bricks and they have walls and doors and windows".

"Do you think they want to build a house here?" asked Sammy squirrel.

"No, I think they want to just visit us. Let's just wait and see what they do" replied Oswald.

The forest animals agreed. They waited and waited but nothing happened. They waited some more but still nothing happened.

Then one morning Oswald felt his leaves quivering on the branches again. The trees on the outer rim of the forest were sending him another message. Lots of little children and two grown-ups were arriving. Oswald was quite curious!

Once the people had arrived, the children sat down in a log circle. The grown-ups were talking about looking after the forest and staying safe in the forest. They were also talking about taking care of the plants and trees. Oswald felt very reassured.

Suddenly, the grown-ups and children started to collect wood, sticks, twigs, leaves and pine-cones from the forest floor. They seemed to be building something. Oswald was amazed to hear them say they were making a mini-beast hotel.

"What is a mini-beast hotel?" asked Melissa mouse.

"It's a sort of house for mini-beasts to live in" said Oswald, "mini-beasts like to live in dark places with lots of nooks and crannies. They seem to be making the hotel out of lots of different natural materials, with lots of little places where mini-beasts like to live".

All the little mini-beasts began to dance and cheer, "Hurray, we will have a special house to live in!" said Wally the woodlouse as he rushed off to pack his things.

When the visitors left the forest, Oswald's little friends couldn't wait to investigate. They crawled inside and inspected every nook and cranny. They each found a place which felt special to them and very soon they were snuggled in their new bug home.

"I think I like the new visitors" said Mrs Ant.

"Yes," said Wally the woodlouse, "they have made a lovely mini-beast house for us!".

Oswald looked down on them and felt happy. The visitors were really kind and made the mini-beasts a home. Oswald felt glad that the people had visited because they had learnt humans, animals and insects live in different places and in different ways. Oswald realised that his forest really did have hidden secrets and he was looking forward to sharing them.

NOTES

NOTES

NOTES

NOTES